KEEP OFF THE GRASS

by Katie Dale and Liam Darcy

W

FRANKLIN WATTS

LONDON•SYDNEY

CHAPTER 1

Simon and Tariq were best friends. Every morning, they rode their bikes to school together.
But one morning, Simon was late. Tariq looked at his watch. If Simon didn't turn up soon, they'd be late for school.

Just then, Simon appeared round the corner.

"Sorry I'm late," he called. "I was practising

football and lost track of time!"

"That's okay," Tariq said, smiling. It was

the big match tomorrow. Simon was their

school's best striker and he had been training

hard for weeks. "But we'd better hurry,

or we'll be late."

"Don't worry, I know a shortcut," Simon said.

"Follow me!"

He cycled across the front lawn of a big house.

"Are you sure?" Tariq said, frowning.

"Come on," Simon called. "I take this shortcut

all the time!"

"Okay," Tariq said, and he started to follow

Simon across the grass.

Suddenly, a window opened, and a man looked out.

"Hey!" he yelled. "Keep off my grass!"

"Sorry," Tariq cried, stopping his bike.

But Simon didn't stop. Instead, he pedalled faster,

leaving Tariq behind.

Tariq turned and cycled back to the path
and took the long way round.

He got to school just as the bell rang.

"What took you so long, slow coach?"

Simon laughed.

Tariq was cross with his friend.

"Why didn't you come back with me?" asked Tariq.

He walked into school without another word
to Simon.

CHAPTER 2

The next morning, Simon was late again.

"Sorry, Tariq!" Simon called. "I forgot my football

boots and had to go back and get them.

I can't play in the big match without them."

"Well at least you've got them now." Tariq said.

"But let's hurry, or we'll be really late."

"Not if we take the shortcut again," Simon grinned,

cycling across the lawn of the big house.

"No, Simon! Stop!" Tariq called. "You'll ruin

the man's lawn!"

"It's only grass. Don't be such a chicken, Tariq,"
Simon laughed.

"Watch out!" Tariq yelled. Simon's bike ran
straight over the beautiful flowers.

"Oops!" Simon said, and pedalled away
as fast as he could.

"Simon, stop," Tariq called. But Simon didn't stop.

Tariq sighed. He couldn't believe Simon had cycled over the man's lawn again. He couldn't believe that Simon had ruined the man's flowers and left without saying sorry. But most of all, he couldn't believe that his best friend had left him behind. Perhaps Simon wasn't much of a friend after all.

As Tariq watched Simon cycle away, he noticed

something falling out of his bag.

"Simon, stop! You've dropped your boots!"

Tariq shouted. But Simon didn't hear him.

He cycled off round the corner, leaving

his boots behind.

"Oh no!" Tariq cried. Simon couldn't play

in the match without his football boots.

And their school wouldn't win if Simon didn't play.

But Tariq couldn't get Simon's boots back without

going on to the man's lawn.

What should he do?

15

CHAPTER 3

Tariq took a deep breath.

He had to get Simon's boots back.

His school and his best friend were relying on him.

But he didn't want to ruin the man's lawn either.

There was only one thing he could do.

Tariq leaned his bike against the fence, and tiptoed

carefully across the lawn.

But just as Tariq reached the football boots,

the front door burst open.

"Freeze!" cried a voice.

Tariq froze as the man ran towards him.

"Look at what you've done to my flowers!"

the man yelled. "I'm going to call the police."

He took out his mobile phone.

"No! Please let me explain," Tariq protested.

"It's not what it looks like."

"But I've caught you on my lawn," said the man.

Tariq was in big trouble – and all because

he'd tried to help Simon. It was so unfair!

CHAPTER 4

"Wait!" called a voice.

Tariq turned to see Simon running across the lawn towards them.

"It's not Tariq's fault!" he cried. "I'm the one who cycled over your lawn and crushed your flowers. Tariq wouldn't come with me. He even tried to stop me."

"Then why is Tariq standing on my lawn now?"

the man asked, suspiciously.

"I dropped my boots." Simon pointed to the football boots in Tariq's hands. "Tariq came to get them for me. He's a good person, and a good friend. I'm the one who should be in trouble, not him."

"Well," said the man. "Tariq has been a good friend. And it's very brave of you to own up. I think you've learned your lesson. Off you go."

"You mean you won't call the police?" said Tariq.

"Not this time," the man said. "But don't let me ever see either of you on my lawn again."

"You won't!" Simon promised.

The two boys hurried to school the long way round and got there just as the bell rang.

"I'm so sorry, Tariq," Simon said. "I should never have taken that shortcut. I should have listened to you. Thank you for getting my boots. You're a good friend." He put his arm over Tariq's shoulder.

"That's okay," Tariq said, smiling. "Thank you for coming back and owning up to squashing the flowers." He put his arm round Simon's shoulder. "You're a good friend, too."

Things to think about

1. Why does Simon go on the man's grass?
2. Why does Tariq turn around and go back to the path?
3. Why do you think Simon comes back when Tariq is caught on the man's lawn?
4. Why does the man change his mind about calling the police?
5. What lessons do you think Simon might have learned?

Write it yourself

One of the themes in this story is being respectful.
Now try to write your own story about a similar theme.

Plan your story before you begin to write it.
Start off with a story map:
• a beginning to introduce the characters and where your story is set (the setting);
• a problem which the main characters will need to fix in the story;
• an ending where the problems are resolved.

Get writing! Try to create interesting characters, not just by telling your reader what they are like, but showing this through their actions. For example, you could show them laughing about something, or running away.

Notes for parents and carers

Independent reading

The aim of independent reading is to read this book with ease. This series is designed to provide an opportunity for your child to read for pleasure and enjoyment. These notes are written for you to help your child make the most of this book.

About the book

This story looks at friendship and respect. Tariq and Simon are best frends, but when Simon is disrespectful about cycling over a man's lawn, Tariq begins to doubt his friend. And when Tariq gets into trouble for Simon's actions, Simon has to prove his friendship by owning up.

Before reading

Ask your child why they have selected this book. Look at the title and blurb together. What do they think it will be about? Do they think they will like it?

During reading

Encourage your child to read independently. If they get stuck on a longer word, remind them that they can find syllable chunks that can be sounded out from left to right. They can also read on in the sentence and think about what would make sense.

After reading

Support comprehension by talking about the story. What happened?
Then help your child think about the messages in the book that go beyond the story, using the questions on the page opposite. Give your child a chance to respond to the story, asking:
Did you enjoy the story and why? Who was your favourite character?
What was your favourite part? What did you expect to happen at the end?

Franklin Watts
First published in Great Britain in 2018
by The Watts Publishing Group

Copyright © The Watts Publishing Group 2018
All rights reserved.

Series Editors: Jackie Hamley and Melanie Palmer
Series Advisors: Dr Sue Bodman and Glen Franklin
Series Designer: Peter Scoulding

A CIP catalogue record for this book is
available from the British Library.

ISBN 978 1 4451 6321 5 (hbk)
ISBN 978 1 4451 6323 9 (pbk)
ISBN 978 1 4451 6322 2 (library ebook)

Printed in China

Franklin Watts
An imprint of
Hachette Children's Group
Part of The Watts Publishing Group
Carmelite House
50 Victoria Embankment
London EC4Y 0DZ

An Hachette UK Company
www.hachette.co.uk

www.franklinwatts.co.uk

FSC
www.fsc.org
MIX
Paper from
responsible sources
FSC® C104740